Mrs. Peachtree's Bicycle

by Erica Silverman

illustrated by Ellen Beier

Simon & Schuster Books for Young Readers

SIMON & SCHUSTER BOOKS FOR YOUNG READERS
An imprint of Simon & Schuster Children's Publishing Division
1230 Avenue of the Americas, New York, NY 10020

Library of Congress Cataloging-in-Publication Data
Silverman, Erica.
Mrs. Peachtree's bicycle / by Erica Silverman ; illustrated by Ellen Beier. — 1st ed.
p.   cm.
Summary: Elderly Mrs. Peachtree persists in her desire to learn to ride a bicycle
and despite many falls says that she will give up only "when cows sing."
ISBN 0-689-80477-6
[1. Old Age—Fiction. 2. Bicycles and bicycling—Fiction.
3. Persistence—Fiction.] I. Beier, Ellen, ill. II. Title.
PZ7.S58625Mrj 1996 [E]—dc20 95-14552

To Deborah Nourse Lattimore, who perseveres—
and helps me do the same
E. S.

To my parents
E. B.

Shadow followed Mrs. Peachtree up one long block and down another.

Walk, stop. Walk, walk, stop. Mrs. Peachtree delivered tea and biscuits all afternoon. At last, her basket was empty. As the sun started to set, she sank down on a stoop to rest.

Shadow hopped into the basket. *"Mrow."*

"Mrow yourself." Mrs. Peachtree rubbed his head. "All this walking is wearing me out. Maybe I ought to trade you in for a horse."

Halfway home, she saw a big circus tent. Festive music filled the air. A noisy crowd thronged through the doors.

Mrs. Peachtree stood at the end of the ticket line. "Not a meow out of you," she whispered.

Soon she was sitting under the big top, resting her feet and sharing peanuts with Shadow. Down in the center ring, a woman was riding a bicycle. Forward and backward she glided in time to the music. She perched on one leg. She balanced on one hand. Then she bowed.

Mrs. Peachtree clapped and clapped. "Shadow," she whispered, "I've got a humdinger of an idea."

The next morning, Mrs. Peachtree hurried to the bicycle shop. "I would like to purchase a wheel," she said.

"This one is quite popular with the ladies," said the shopkeeper.

"A tricycle?" Mrs. Peachtree frowned. "Won't that be too slow?"

"What's your hurry?" said the shopkeeper.

Mrs. Peachtree pointed to a bicycle with two equal-size tires. "I want that one."

"Do you know how to wheel?" asked the shopkeeper.

"Don't be a goose!" said Mrs. Peachtree. "Any fool can move her legs up and down."

She walked the bicycle outside and climbed on. "See. Nothing to it." But then she put her feet on the pedals. She teetered. She tottered. She wavered and swayed. "Oh, fiddle-faddle!" cried Mrs. Peachtree. And down she went!

"Give up?" said the shopkeeper.

"When cows sing!" snapped Mrs. Peachtree. "That's when I'll give up." She walked her bicycle home.

In front of her tea shop, Mrs. Peachtree tried again. "Really, how hard can it be?" she muttered. Slowly she put one foot on each pedal.

She teetered. She tottered. She wavered and swayed.

The milkman caught her before she fell.

"Ladies can't wheel," he said. "It takes too much concentration."

"Is that so?" said Mrs. Peachtree.

The next day Mrs. Peachtree entered the City Riding Academy.

"Ladies' hall to the left," said the doorman.

"Fifty cents, please," said the clerk.

"Concentrate," said the instructor.

Mrs. Peachtree inched her way slowly around the big room. Someone zipped by. "Look at that!" she said, pointing.

She teetered. She tottered. She wavered and swayed. "Oh, fiddle-faddle!" cried Mrs. Peachtree. And down she went.

"Don't let anyone distract you," said the instructor.

Mrs. Peachtree stared straight ahead and pedaled.

"Better," said the instructor. "Now go home and practice."

All week Mrs. Peachtree rolled up and down the block. Shadow watched. So did the milliner.

"Aren't you too old for that?" said the milliner.

Mrs. Peachtree studied her own reflection as she pedaled by a shop window. "No," she replied. And down she went, into a flower cart.

"Won't you give up?" asked the milliner.

"When cows sing," snapped Mrs. Peachtree.

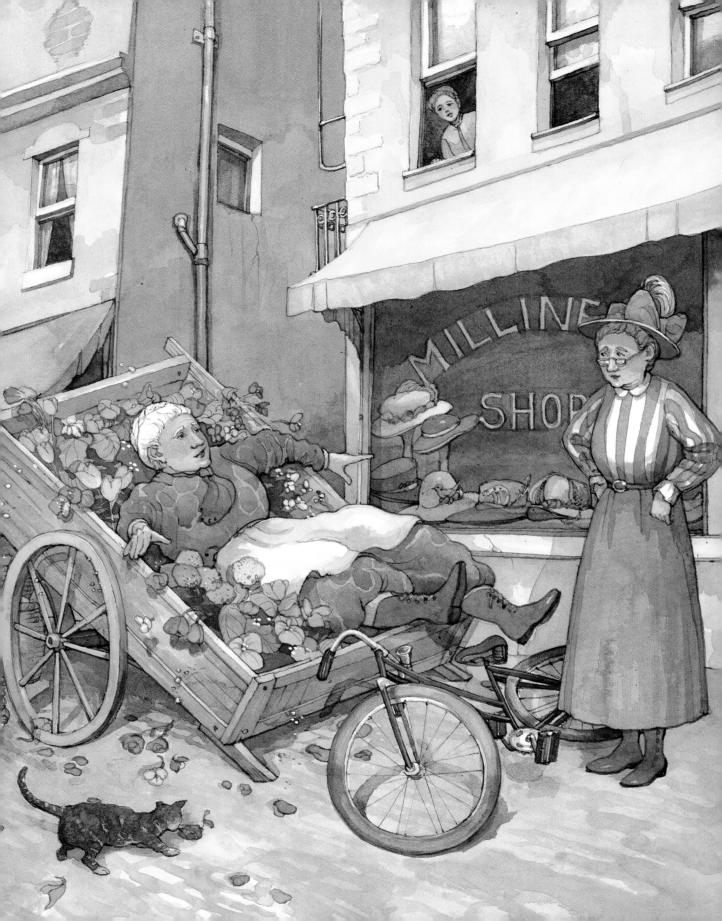

The next morning Mrs. Peachtree practiced in the rain.

"Have you lost your marbles?" called the iceman.

"Not yet." Mrs. Peachtree turned and waved.

She teetered. She tottered. She wavered and swayed. "Oh, fiddle-faddle!" cried Mrs. Peachtree. And down she went, into a puddle.

"Mrs. Peachtree, when will you give up?" said the iceman.

"When cows sing," snapped Mrs. Peachtree. "Right, Shadow?"

"*Mrow*," said Shadow.

Every morning, before she opened the store, Mrs. Peachtree practiced. Every afternoon, after she closed the store, she plodded all over the city delivering tea and biscuits. Every evening she soaked her feet in hot water.

Finally, one afternoon Mrs. Peachtree attached a basketful of tea and biscuits to the back of her bicycle. "I've practiced enough," she announced. "It's time to make my deliveries by wheel." She put another basket on the front. "Our walking days are over!" Shadow leaped into the empty basket.

Mrs. Peachtree rode up Eighth Avenue. Carefully, she turned the corner.

"Hey, lady, out of my way!" A vegetable wagon clattered close behind her. Too close!

"Oh, no!" cried Mrs. Peachtree. Down she went.

The horse bolted. The wagon tipped. Cabbages and onions went rolling and bouncing all over the cobblestoned street.

Wagon drivers clanged their bells and shouted.

A policeman strode over. "You wheelers are a menace to the road," he scolded.

Slowly Mrs. Peachtree stood up. Her legs shook. Her shoulders slumped. "Oh, Shadow. The cows are singing." She rubbed her sore arm. "Shadow?" The basket was empty. "Shadow?" Mrs. Peachtree looked all around.

A big dog was pawing at one of the wagon wheels.

"*Mrrooooowwwww!*" Something streaked out from under the wagon. The dog raced after it.

"Shadow!" Mrs. Peachtree jumped onto her bicycle.

Her heart raced. On and on she rode, past horses and carts, wagons and carriages, trolleys and cabriolets.

"Lady, stop!" called the policeman.

Mrs. Peachtree reached the park. She saw Shadow scramble up a tree.

The dog circled the trunk, sniffing and snarling.

Mrs. Peachtree jumped off her bicycle. "Go away, dog!"
She stomped her foot.

The dog lowered its tail and slunk off.

"Here, kitty," cooed Mrs. Peachtree. "You can come down now."

Shadow crawled into her outstretched arms. "*Mrow.*"

"Mrow yourself." Mrs. Peachtree held him tight.

The policeman ran up behind her. "You were going too fast, lady. I have to give you a ticket for scorching."

Mrs. Peachtree laughed. "I was just about to give up. And now I'm a scorcher." She held the ticket proudly. "Patrolman, sir, can you wheel?"

The policeman shook his head. "No, ma'am."

"Well, if you ever decide to try, just concentrate. And don't let anyone tell you you can't do it."

"*Mrow*," said Shadow.

"Mrow yourself," said Mrs. Peachtree. And she put Shadow back in the basket and pedaled away.